The World Afloat

Also by M.A.C. Farrant

Non-Fiction
My Turquoise Years
The Secret Lives of Litterbugs and Other True Stories

Novels
The Strange Truth About Us: A Novel of Absence*

Short Stories
Sick Pigeon
Raw Material
Altered Statements
Word of Mouth
What's True, Darling
Girls Around the House
Darwin Alone in the Universe*
The Breakdown So Far*
Down the Road to Eternity: New and Selected Fiction*

Play
My Turquoise Years

* Available from Talonbooks

The World Afloat

Miniatures

M.A.C. Farrant

Talonbooks

Talonbooks
P.O. Box 2076, Vancouver, British Columbia, Canada V6B 3S3
www.talonbooks.com

First printing: 2014

Typeset in Scala and printed and bound in Canada
Printed on 100% post-consumer recycled paper

Interior and cover design by Typesmith

Cover illustration by Catrin Welz-Stein, Catrinwelzstein.blogspot.com

Talonbooks gratefully acknowledges the financial support of the Canada Council for the Arts, the Government of Canada through the Canada Book Fund, and the Province of British Columbia through the British Columbia Arts Council and the Book Publishing Tax Credit.

Library and Archives Canada Cataloguing in Publication

Farrant, M. A. C. (Marion Alice Coburn), author
        The world afloat / M.A.C. Farrant.

Short stories.
Issued in print and electronic formats.
ISBN 978-0-88922-838-2 (pbk.).—ISBN 978-0-88922-839-9 (epub)

        I. Title.

PS8561.A76W674 2014   C813'.54   C2014-900467-2

                                                C2014-900468-0

For Bill and Anna

Contents

Part One

Part Two

Part Three

Part One

Tick Tock

He was walking down the street.

He dropped dead.

He was a watchmaker.

Which street?

Young Man with Leaflets

The young man standing at my front door offers to safeguard my heart. "I already have a couple of people doing that," I tell him. "One of them is out back, sharpening the axe."

I know he wants me to commit to his superhero for the next fifty years. But I already have a superhero.

"Her bra size," I say, "is three times larger than a normal woman's and she has this incredible desire to dress like a slut. A lot of men don't like her because she's so stunning and monumental. Girls and women," I add, "tend not to be interested in overly muscled guys with thick necks and big chains beating each other up. Is your superhero one of those?"

"Jesus Christ!" he says.

"Well, mine's such an icon," I say. "She's just like Marilyn Monroe. Women dress up like her for Halloween and at conventions. Do you dress up like yours?"

He doesn't get to answer because the phone rings, Bizzy barks, my superhero shoots through the door in her blue satin shorts, and Manny Moss comes round the side of the house swinging his axe.

The sun flickers like it is shorting out and the young man backs away. The scene is a bit funny in a conceptual kind of way. I think, Here is a moment of perfection, one where you want everything to stop. ☙

Tanya's Muffins

I was having a really intense time with Parker, constantly taking my clothes off. I didn't have an issue with this because his family was going through some heavy counselling. So it felt like being naked in his office was helpful for reducing his stress.

"Tanya," he said, "don't expect deep messages or metaphors from me. It is what it is. It's a ride."

I was okay with that. I got to sort of pop in and pop out and that was great and very relaxing. I thought, Probably the best mindset is to think of this as a project; just whittle away at it and see where it goes.

So every day I'd deliver muffins to the pretty little secretaries and then visit Parker in his office. And every day he'd pull out his spring-loaded measuring thing and we'd measure away for twenty minutes or so.

But then he was like, "This is terrible, this is horrible." He was really choked, right? And all I'd done for something new was put my sword on his desk.

The secretaries frickin' loved it. They were like little brown birds that had been shoved from the feeder and this touched me deeper than skin.

The sword's a ceremonial one from the U.S. Naval Academy. It's delicate, meant to impress, and is usually worn with a dress uniform. But I'm not trying to make people think or feel. I just like the way the sword goes so good with my tits. ⮑

How the Summer Wash Deserts Us

Fall arrives and the summer wash prepares for its annual migration. Bathing suits, towels, light dresses, and shirts unhook themselves from clotheslines. They become agitated like birds. And rebellious, deciding where and when they'll be hung. From the trees near the beach, it turns out. You can catch them but it's a wasted effort.

Because when the rains come, the wash heads north for the frozen shores of Labrador. That's something to watch – shirts flapping towards the far horizon, dresses gliding alongside.

But wait! Their departure signals the return of the wash from Ecuador. We'd forgotten about that, about the pink and yellow socks that will soon be wintering on our lines, their cheerfulness hauling us through another dark season. ∽

The Day Is Old Enough to Have Complications

In the morning there are eyelid kisses and Uncle Roger
saying, "Let's visit spring today." And we'll go to the mall
and stand beside tables filled with colourful tank tops
from China and just inhale the smell.

But best are the shoe stores. That's where you hear
girl clerks asking why Brandon and Jerome aren't
more important than discount shoes, or hear long
conversations about love and the problems with Father.

There's a belief here that those who die shopping
return to the mall as ghosts. On sale days you can
see them creeping about at night as if it were a dark,
smoking wood.

The bored clerks stationed in The Bay's menswear
department know this. That's where old men in
beige slacks go to die. It's where we're headed now,
Uncle Roger having developed a sudden interest in
tube socks. ❧

A True Story about Normal Circumstances Including Some Insane Footage

I'm notorious for doing things. One of my challenges is to be not boring. It's like you are real but only if you're interesting enough to keep people awake. Otherwise, you might as well work in a nursing home.

It's naive to think you deserve to be where you are. It could go away real fucking fast. People come apart and shit happens. Then all of a sudden that thing you thought would last forever goes away and you've got the dead eyes of a zombie.

So to help people out I organize this annual event, this zombie walk after-party basically. Hundreds of zombies wander downtown and then they just shamble about mindlessly. I look at it, like, half-life can be difficult, so I've added some wonderful heartfelt elements for the zombies to engage with, such as gas-filled buzzards and neck and shoulder massage.

For years and years there were limitations on what the zombies could do. It was, like, "Nope, no acting weird on city streets." But times now are a bit brighter and shinier. Now it's more like, "Oh, we like the community feel of where you have come to."

Mainly, though, I want the zombies to be real, but only if they're positive. So I kind of do want them to fake it if they're feeling negative. I don't want to show zombies as pissed off. Maybe if we keep that perspective we'll be like clouds today, almost like a birthday.

And, yes, that is a small Asian woman in a birdcage. ～

Everyone's Life Is a Labyrinth

There are many corners to turn. This is something people are doing: turning corners. You have to turn a corner if you want to move on.

I don't remember how I came to turn the corner leading to Glenda's party. But hanging up my coat I noticed three perfect cabbages growing on the back wall of the closet. I reasoned that cabbage seeds had been shat there by a closet-flying bird of some sort. I remember wondering if the cabbages were a sign that I would soon be moving on.

I did, but only to the kitchen where Glenda pulled open the cutlery drawer to show me what was inside: several large, clean, white potatoes sitting on a cushion of dirt. Each potato was attached to the dirt by a potato umbilical cord. That makes sense, I remember thinking, and also that each potato was a singular and exquisite object. I wanted one of those potatoes badly.

But before I could offer Glenda the dried tangerine in my purse in exchange for a potato, I turned another corner and moved into her living room where three elderly musicians were leaning against the wall complaining about their hearing aids. "Only eighty percent reception at best," said the one dressed in black. The musicians were attached by a nest of cords to a large sound system. I understood there would be no more turning corners for them.

I think it was then that I noticed the live tomatoes hanging like streamers from the ceiling and came to understand that at Glenda's party umbilical cords were everywhere, like a theme. And that they were feeding the living, the live potatoes, and even me because something was tugging on my arm.

It was then I remembered my dog. He was attached to me by a lead made of wool. Or perhaps I was attached to him. In any case, my dog was made entirely of brown wool – little trotting feet, little ears.

I have my dog, I remember thinking, and together we will turn another corner and reach somewhere else. I can't remember if I was also made of wool but I felt sure we were moving in the right direction. ❧

A Frothy Moment Keeps the World Afloat

Thin frowns at the black sky outside the kitchen window.
You can't tell which is blacker – Thin's face or the sky.
    So I say lightly, "Compared to the little hairy thing
I just shooed out the door, I'm a big bald thing."
    "Not bald enough," Thin says, hinting of paradise lost.
    He wears rue to the dinner table like an old black coat.
    In high school I majored in perkiness and keeping
your mister happy and keeping the moment frothy so
I know what to do.
    We're eating sausages, salad, raw broccoli, celery.
For dessert I've planned one chocolate cookie apiece.
    "Guess what?" I say, putting my training to work.
"There's a surprise in your salad!"
    "I hope it's lysergic acid," Thin says, and begins poking
through his lettuce. He looks like a bored boy pulling
apart a birthday cake for dimes. What he finds are the
surprise cashews.
    The candles flicker in merriment if not in
transcendence.
    Unlike me, Thin is hairy. I have a bald, pinched
little face that I've learned to thrust bravely forward.
Sometimes I can even make it grin at Thin, like now. ⌒

The State

I have always taken pride in my defensive manoeuvres
but Thursday morning I was caught off guard. Dwain
was suddenly standing before me in the mall looking
bad. I hadn't noticed his approach because I'd been
transfixed by a 70% Off Everything sign. So I caught
the state from Dwain. He said he hadn't slept a wink the
night before and saying this was enough to infect me.
That's how this state begins, through airborne words.

For a while I thought I might have escaped the state.
Even when Sherry giggled and pulled off the bedcovers
I thought this was true. But the state was in its incubation
stage. And I knew I was in trouble when for no reason
my thrust got sore. One moment it was fine, the next,
raw as a rash. So I said to Sherry, "Slow down, my thrust
is sore," and with a grunt she slid to the far side of the
bed. I lay there and thought, Fuck, I would be staring at
the walls for hours now; the sound of no sound was
going to be loud.

Around midnight the state went to my head. Every
stupid, heartless thing I'd ever done took up residence
there. All the lies and deceits, every pathetic bid for
attention filled me with disgust.

By two forty the state overtook me completely. I turned
grey and did the Swedish belching thing. Thinking
everything in life is worth precisely as much as a belch
is what the Swedish belching thing is all about.

A second night of the state can be hell. Dwain was
probably experiencing the aftermath of night two when

I had seen him at the mall. He'd shrunk in size and looked crushed, burned, and sawed.

So here is the situation. Tonight I can expect to lie in bed like a skeleton and await the flesh and sinew of demons to clothe me. Sherry will be wearing her sleep mask and earplugs and lying as far away from me as possible while I will be lost in the dark, unfathomable rooms of my soul. And my thrust will still be sore. But around daybreak I'm hoping the state will subside. This is because I'll be spending the night practising a rigorous antidote. This consists of nothing more than developing my determination that I never become so lost I get religious. I will repeat this thought over and over like a mantra. It's the insomniac's best defence. ⌒

A Noise in the World

Being October the dinner party theme was dead leaves
and orange candles.

I was sitting across the table from Scott, my handsome
neighbour and host. Beneath the table, and out of sight,
Scott was massaging my right foot, which I'd placed in
his lap as a party gift. And while he was massaging my
foot, and paying particular attention to the base of
my big toe, which was causing waves of pleasure to
flood my brain, his wife, Lori – she's an artist in wool –
was showing off the latest sweater she had knit. It was
off-white in colour and had a design of off-white leaves
that were raised and nubbly.

"The sweater," she said, "is like bas-relief sculpture
only the medium is wool not stone. My work is a noise
in the world."

And everyone admired her noise.

I was thinking, while still enjoying the foot massage
and registering that Scott had moved on to my instep,
which he was kneading like a slab of bread dough,
I was thinking that we all go through the same dramas,
we look in the mirror and say, What happened? Once
we had muscles and slowly they deteriorate, which
meant that I was actually observing how we were all
pretty old at the party despite the distracting jewellery
and the cleavage and the exercised bodies everyone had.

Then, as if to counter my unexpressed thought and
to keep the world afloat a little longer, Lori asked me
to retell an amusing story I had told on a previous visit
and everyone looked at me thirstily. But because of the

foot massage that was still in progress my mind went blank and I couldn't remember how the story went. It was something about Mother feeding me moods in her kitchen, or maybe it was Scotch and cigarettes.

I was puzzling over this when Scott, with his significant great qualities, indicated by a squeeze of my heel that I would soon be delivered of mental struggle. So I said, "Perhaps if I went home for a copy of the story I could read it to you," knowing full well that squirrels and possibly wild rabbits would be prowling the suburban streets that lead to my house and that Scott might offer to protect me on the walk, which is exactly what he did.

Needless to say blood rushed everywhere then, especially when I was putting on my shoes and coat and watching Scott grab his high-powered flashlight. Anticipation, you could say, lit up the mud room as if someone had stuck a finger in my eye and I was seeing, not the faces of my friends, but fairy lights.

And then it occurred to me as we were saying goodbye and telling everyone we wouldn't be long, that the universe wanted to be tough for Scott and me. It was a special kind of exhilarating toughness, and there was no better feeling. A feeling so emotional and stark it left me believing I could even seduce a mirror. A feeling like I was a fifty-nine-year-old woman newly returned from studying with Sigmund Freud and now I knew everything. ⌒

When the Last Straw Is a Tomato

There was a turkey dinner with everyone in the living room waiting, including four babies and seven kids. Elaine and Axel were in the kitchen getting things ready. As usual, Axel had delegated Elaine to make the green salad, which caused her to feel, she said, so seventy-nine, which is exactly what she was. But she made the salad because Axel was making everything else. He always did.

"No one wants salad at a turkey dinner," she often said. "It's all about turkey, stuffing, potatoes, cranberry sauce, and the big man getting the praise."

She'd pushed her walker to the fridge and got the lettuce and started tearing it apart at the counter and filling the salad bowl. Then Axel, who was making gravy and had one of her striped tea towels stuck in the front of his pants as an apron, kept on at her about when was she going to add the tomatoes to the salad.

"You don't add tomatoes until the last minute, otherwise the salad gets mushy," she said.

But Axel wouldn't stop nagging about the tomatoes. For a full half hour he nagged, so she threw a tomato at him. Until then, she said, she had been one of those people who go along with things too much.

Later that night after everyone had left, Axel was still going on about the way she had let the salad get mushy. "Because you told me to put the tomatoes in too soon," Elaine said, and then she said she wanted a divorce. "Finish your living without me."

Later that month she moved in with her daughter. That's all. The tomato she threw hit Axel on his old shoulder. The look on his face. ~

We Appreciate Him Now

He was standing at the table saw in his other form as Uncle Ernie. There was the smell of sawdust about the workshop, and I think something dramatic in nature like his being ahead of his time.

I was eleven years old and had been harbouring the worst kind of big deal, raging against the unfairness of my aunt.

Ernie didn't appreciate people empty of purposeful activity, which described me much of the time.

"Stop jabbering," he said. He was short and bald and wore green work clothes. "Start collecting elastic bands and string. Start sorting, counting, and storing."

He meant I should take my mind off my situation.

I saw the saw in his shop. He knew what he was talking about. His mind was a workbench. For years he'd been rolling silver foil into balls. My aunt was a hectoring person.

He wasn't offering me advice in the form of perversity, but as a general kindness, a helpful hint. I thought about elastic bands and string and calmed way down.

I'm supposing Ernie was unhappy in his life's work, which was being a janitor. I'm supposing he was unhappy with his dominant wife and that this caused him to be in danger of his mind cracking open and leaking out the way a dropped egg does.

But that didn't seem to happen. Instead he had those silver balls, which stayed intact. Over the years he rolled this activity over my aunt's objections, mostly.

"Stop doing that," she'd yell. That did happen when Ernie died. After the funeral she found seven silver balls in his workshop.

I think he was ahead of his time with his emptied mind, the result of perpetually smoothing a piece of silver foil and adding it to a larger and larger ball. Out there in his cold workshop he was like an adept practising mind control. He got the foil from cigarette packages and wrapped chocolates. Everything he did was done slowly and with purpose.

I'm still in there with the sawdust smell of him! ⁓

His Trouble

He's exhausted from living among boarded-up houses
in Mesa, Arizona. And now a thirty-day notice has
been stapled to his front door as if that doesn't deliver
a person to the bottom rung of the ladder.

He's Canadian, belly-rounded, wife-dead, alone.
The situation proceeds from there. "Fuck it, and fuck it
again," he says, meaning the world and all his trouble.

He's filing hardship claims with the U.S. government
but being sixty-eight and an alien – good luck. He's
got TV and drinking his Canadian pension and bad
veins and no medical and trouble with his back and
the times that were.

I sent him not much money for his good luck.

One time he said he was like Christ because he never
aged. "Like Christ," he said. This was during the years
his wallet was full of cash due to his correct opinions
about horses. ~

Couple Sucks Same Candy

Culturally, for Ron and me, Shoppers Drug Mart is all there is. So when the cashier called me *Lovey* while handing over my bag of toilet paper and shampoo I felt happy, fulfilled. I was still feeling that way when an older man holding an apple pie behind me in the checkout line at Safeway tapped me on the shoulder. "Look at that," he said, pointing at a headline in the *National Enquirer* – "Jen Pregnant and Alone."

"Aren't you glad you're not famous?"

I thought about this on our drive home and decided, yes, I'm glad we're not famous. Because imagine a man on a motorcycle taking a picture of Ron and me sharing the hard candy Ron found in his jacket pocket. It must have been there for years. A lime one wrapped in clear plastic. We didn't think twice. I sucked the first half and Ron finished it off. But after that I saw the headline – "Couple Sucks Same Candy" – and knew the world would find us disgusting. So full marks for anonymity.

At home we continued our afternoon by pulling apart the jigsaw puzzle from Christmas. Only the sky, the head of a fish, and a few trees were finished and it was just about March. The puzzle had become a burden. You could spend hours and hours and only find one matching piece so that pretty soon night would be falling with supper nowhere in sight. It was a revelation when I told myself that some things in life could go unfinished and Ron agreed. Actually, pretty much everything can go unfinished, we decided, and especially the jigsaw puzzle, which we had come to hate.

There was a bowl on the side table filled with the pieces of a large bear that would never inhabit its shape. They went into the jigsaw box, along with the broken sky, the head of a fish that would have been in the bear's paw, and the several small trees.

"I wouldn't mind taking my life apart and returning it to an attractive box," I said – mindlessly, I suppose, because of not having to finish the puzzle – and Ron said, "Think again." "Oh right," I said. "I'd forgotten about that."

So I thought instead how happy I am with our home and all the machinations thereof. And with my goldfish, Hilda, who gives me no trouble, and with my little commercials for the family, who frequently do: our girls with their toenail palace, and our son, Boyd, who still wants to be an astronaut, and my brother, Doug, who's never paid me back for totalling my car in 1979, a sweet little Volkswagen. And I thought about Nature. How every once in a while there'll be a day with sun. And a few clouds. Ones the way I always want them to be. Clouds like shampoo foam. ᵔ

Juliet Nearly Succumbs

That Juliet is beginning an adventure is established in
the opening moments of the story. That her husband
will be absent from the foreign city where Juliet was to
meet him is also established. Tariq, his much younger
colleague, will entertain her in his absence.

Well, then, what is expected begins unfolding with
the sudden arrival of Juliet's older legs wearing dresses
when before they'd been covered with stiff beige slacks.

Luckily, her face at fifty-six is without jowls and her
neck remains intact. Unlike us she will keep. Unlike us
music will play around her everywhere she goes. This
music tells us that even though husbands may be best
she is now mostly with Tariq – on foot, in a car, on a
train or a boat.

Beneath glaring sunlight, then, and in city streets,
Juliet wanders with Tariq. Her dresses are yellow, black,
or turquoise culminating in a flowered dress, which
is worn when Tariq clasps a silver necklace around
her neck at a street stall. She has now, we know, been
anointed goddess and is no longer small like us.

Later, there will be white wine and quiet sweating on
her hotel balcony and we will sweat, too. But still there
will be no touching, though many warm looks will be
exchanged and Tariq will continue to softly grab her
name whenever he can.

Her name means *Seems young though she is old*. His
name means *Desert flecks in bright sunlight.*

His name flutters our breaths, certainly, but the
absent-husband days will soon come to an end, we fear.

But not yet! Not before Juliet and Tariq visit the pyramids wearing worthy black slacks. Together they will look longingly at the desert and at the empty sky with birds flying overhead. Then they will take more languid walks through the story. This walking and looking, we know, is the prelude to finding the door to removing Juliet's clothes.

These facts have pale skin and clear blue eyes and dark skin and wetly brown eyes and once giant breasts in the form of small pyramids, which strike us as an authentic representation of beauty.

Into the distance, then, we yearn for Juliet and Tariq to walk naked and in time to the sitar music that was playing at the mosque earlier in the day when Juliet delicately removed her shoes.

Too soon, though, her husband returns. His name is Mark, which means *Short, rugged, lovable, and not unhandsome.*

The music that is now playing sounds wistful and does not even begin to console us over Juliet's loss of Tariq. ~

Bit Part / Twin Peaks

They don't say why it is happening. Why the falls keep falling. Why the young woman wrapped in see-through plastic is found by the side of the river. Why men gather there to poke at her body amazed.

They tell us through music that the most marvellous flowers become organs of decay. Then shoot the days and nights with a soft kind of evil.

Black light, grey light, cloud, intermittent rain, a slight wind as if ghosts were drifting by; these things calm us for the next peaking moments.

As the sawmill burns; the crazed phantom overpowers the lawyer; the dreamtime midget acts like a dream; the beautiful waitress is steadily abused; the Log Lady cradles her piece of wood and speaks movingly of transcendence.

Throughout there's the sombre music, the swollen river, and then, finally, me showing the sheriff a good time in the seedy motel. They say I'm the one-eyed Jack disguised as a schoolgirl. I'm wearing white knee socks, a black patch over my left eye.

They don't say why I am happy. ～

Nothing Could Be More Like Life
Than What We Were Watching

"This is it," you said. "This is what hope becomes after you lose it."

We were staring at a field of weeds and brown grass. A worn path travelled across it.

"That path," I said, "has seen better days, as have I."

"That field," you said, but didn't finish.

Then a dog wandered into the centre of the field and peed. He was a harmless old thing, used to being unmolested and fed.

Someone large and wearing a black cape and hood came next and strode headlong down the path as if on an urgent mission, passing by the dog that now lay cowering on its back.

"Lost hope must look like a grainy black-and-white film," you said, "with death striding across every frame."

A woman's screams were then heard from a house across the field. We knew she was young, Swedish, beautiful, and had ground glass into her vagina because her tiresome husband in 1888 was once again demanding his tiresome right ...

"There are so many things you would never think to tell anyone," I said. ↝

He Could Be Droll

My father could make stew last a week, a razor blade
last six months, and disdain for a second marriage last
a lifetime. He once told me how to make scrambled eggs.
"Beat the eggs in the driveway with a wooden spoon,"
he said. "That way violence stays out of the kitchen."

From the time I was very young he lived in quiet
buildings, among ghost-like people. I had to tiptoe
through airless hallways to find his rooms. Inside we
spoke in whispers. It was like a game. "Pretend we're
mice," he'd say.

His kitchen was small, clean, well ordered.

Unlike that other kitchen where a bowl of gravy was
thrown against the kitchen wall and my father fled
through the door. ∼

Autumn Idyll

Byron's manhood often occurred spontaneously. "When
did spawning salmon become a religion?" he asked.
   "When we became celebrants of dead ends," I said.
   That day anticipation stirred in Byron like a poplar
about to shed its leaves. "Let's make a pilgrimage," he said.
   So hand in hand we walked into the yellow light.
Me, calmly like a queen among rabble; Byron, with his
damp anxiety.
   The salmon climbing those wooded stairs to die. The
velocity of the water just so ... ∿

Steak Soup

We were poor and plain. There wasn't much about us;
we were run-of-the-mill invisibles. Looking back this was
young and sweet. We had babies, a shaky car, lost jobs.
Obviously, we were at the start of the problem years.

So we took the insurance, cut back, and just kind of
winged it. And all around people showed mad support.
If we were invited out and served steak we brought
home the bones and had soup for a week. We didn't
mind. It was "I'm me," and "You're singing," and it was
all pretty exciting.

Some nights we'd dress up like we were going to a party
and then head for the living room. Friends would be there
with a six-pack and a plate of cake. It was good to celebrate
the curtain staying risen. It was impossible not to be alive.
We danced to "Mellow Apples," that Roy Rogers tune,
winding the cassette back with a pencil to play the song
again. I felt so cowboy. I was on some kind of frontier.
Your mother kept bags of Mars bars and a case of Scotch
at her apartment. A wise woman; we loved to visit!

Now and then the car blew up. We learned to
experience this as random fireworks.

And once when we were scavenging through the lost-
and-found bin at the kids' elementary school, a beautiful
Depression-era feeling overcame me – steadfast,
fireplace warm. From that time on I registered my
ability to create this feeling and offered myself copious
thanks. My narratives kept us going. It was vital to weave
complex storylines. We were living a long-haul text, part
of which was hoping our luck would change.

It finally did after the kids had left, when we'd begun
to love certain institutions. So what's the problem now?
Why the sour face? We're still here, on some kind of
last frontier, aren't we? And you've got these spanking
new dentures. ～

The Freshest Look Is an Odd Shape

At three I was imitating and doing fun little skits for the family. At five I knew, Okay, this is something I like. At eight I was pretend crying in front of the mirror and my mom was like, "Oh boy, here we go, we know what's up for Tyler." At ten I was taking trapeze lessons and swinging by my knees on the bar Uncle Jay rigged up in the backyard. At thirteen I was wearing yellow because yellow is the colour of a high I.Q. And by high school I was perceived as having these quirks and doing weird things. I wore a rooster costume to school dances a few times. I did handstands that came completely out of nowhere, like in a bank lineup or ordering a Blizzard at Dairy Queen. And I talked outside of humans like a poet. About how clouds that hate are the ones that cry, how mountains feel awkward all the time, how paintings really want to be touched. And this was just ordinary living.

The school counsellor, Mr. Rash, said, "Is your world the one where the only big welcome is to win the grand prize, the $100,000 cash, the $25,000 gift coupon to the Brick, and the new Chevrolet Trax?"

"No," I said. "It's the one where I'm like a little Arabian horse. Just perfect." ∼

Orange as a Ball

We leave Keith in the van working on his bag of jujubes.
He's difficult after an outing, wanting to be alone.

Marilyn, on the other hand, can't wait to get inside,
already she's got *American Idol* on. Maybe it'll improve
her mood. Here's hoping. She was foul on the trip
home, hating the boots she got at Value Village. But
I know the real reason for her mood is Norman, her
undertaker boyfriend. He's got some other woman
pregnant. Marilyn is thirty-eight years old and having
not much of a life.

Her twin Mona's the same. We picked her up soaking
wet by the side of the road. I said, "What the hell
happened to you?" And she said, "Man, whenever I see a
loose animal it makes me feel so weird!" So that's Mona.

Then there's my sister, Lena – Keith and the twins'
mother. She's doing better now. She likes her new
hospital bed. Lex, her ex, set it up in the living room using
his good arm. Nothing's the matter with Lena as far as
I can tell, just wants to be the centre of attention. Well,
who doesn't? Keith's been the centre of attention for years.
I see he's out of the van now playing by himself under
the back porch light. One-person baseball using the dog's
bone as a bat and a skull painted orange as a ball.

As for me, I'm the aunt living in the basement. I go
to the mirror; I look at my melancholy face. And I say to
myself, Lighten up for Christ's sake, think of something
good. So here is something good. We're not afraid of
Disney anymore. The good news is Disney's not going
to put mouse ears on the Coca-Cola sign. It's fine.
Everybody's calmed down about Disney. ~

Some of the Many Reasons

There were spiritual difficulties. She simply would
not drain away the nonsense. She had no outpourings
of generous beauty. She halted all discussions of our
future beyond sharing my bed. I did not have excellent
teeth and was a ruin for her mother. I was felled by
her demonstration of the verb *whine*. The stars when
I looked at them seemed irregular. I was always stopping
short of bodily anguish. Her hectoring had no halting.
Nature did not have a command of words and remained
uncommunicative. There was just the cool moon and
me with a heart of oak.

The one who has it right is the guy standing on the
Six-Mile Highway happily shouting, "I'm leaving another
woman on her front porch shaking her fist at me!" A guy
like me with ice-cream stains on his shirt, who might
otherwise spend many hours alone and loving his dog.

"Sparky, I'm back!" ∽

The Times Felt Like Doctoring

Dr. B. told me to open my heart wide. I did and he saw
stuff in there he can't unsee. Like soft outrage hiding
my inner dwarf and the fact that I am quite sick about
vanished days, the ones that were all about me.

Dr. B. talked quietly and massaged my hands. He's
highly skilled and carries out established procedures.

"My feeling," I said, "is hard and cold and physical. It's
like I'm your plumber; I'm one-track; step out of my way,
I'll fix your toilet. It's like when I go to the mall they have
to close the mall down."

A blister on my hand burst and blood spewed over
Dr. B.'s tan mohair suit. I noticed his pants had a perfect
crease. He looked like a giant. He was slim, regal. He
was elegant. His eyes scrunched and there were wrinkles
in his forehead.

Dr. B. is really smart with his rescues such as when
my lack of confidence gets me into jams. He told me to
keep singing so he could stay awake. He said, "A worthy
goal is – why not aim for the top of your competence?"
He said, "Sleep well tonight," and wished me great
happiness. He said, "Here are some dog cookies to
take home and, if you don't have a dog, give them
to someone deserving." ∿

Feathers, Dirt, Bugs

It happened earlier in the day. I got into a fight with Angela and freaked myself out. Come bedtime we were like two cats curled on separate pillows.

Then the raven, its darkness flying through the open window. It settled in bed between us. The raven's beak inches from my neck. The raven interrupting my dream about lifting a bus over my head to throw at Angela.

But the bird's presence charmed me. I thought, Hey, a raven has got into bed with us, maybe we're being honoured in some way. It took up a lot of room. When I touched its wing it felt sharp like the teeth of a chainsaw.

Still, it was really hard to understand where the raven fit into the family drama. I tried to think about that. How ravens, along with crows, magpies, and jays, belong to the family of birds called *Corvidae*. How I belong to the group of people with the thinnest skin. How ravens are more intelligent than border collies. How I've often thought Bandit was smarter than me.

Angela didn't know the raven was in bed with us because she didn't wake up. She spent the night curled and battling on the other side of the bed. With the raven lying stiff between us. Some people have even less, I thought.

For the first time it seemed funny about my name being Matt. It was like I'm matted together with Angela and it was painful being pulled apart and then to have a large bird lying between us.

Angela and the raven slept but I couldn't.
Crows shooting laser beams out of their eyes like
superheroes – that I could understand. But a raven
using my bed as a nest?

Maybe I'd caused the raven to materialize, I thought,
it being a crazy, negative reaction to fighting with
Angela. Maybe the raven was the dark side of me.

I guess I drifted off. In the early morning a bunch of
burly, tattooed men threw tomatoes at me. Which woke
me up. Angela woke up, too, and pulled the covers back.
The raven startled and flew out the window. Angela
screamed, said something about my bizarre pets, and
fled to the bathroom.

There wasn't much of the raven left to prove it had
even been there: a couple of feathers, some dirt, and
several grey bugs. I think it was the bugs crawling across
the white sheet that got Angela screaming. Bugs the
size of earwigs.

It might be utopian, but I like to believe in the great
zone where two people can reach out and communicate
while under the same covers. Minus a raven.

I decided to use the bus I'd dreamed about earlier
in an abstract and poetic way. I'd tell Angela that when
she came out of the bathroom. I'd say I wasn't trying to
go over her head. I'd say I was fighting with her to say
just anything. ～

The Moment Contracts

She is dancing to Latin music in the kitchen – salsa with
the tomatoes, tango with the broom. Sixty-five beats per
minute. But something is wrong. There's a man who is
striding past her with a frown on his face and a book in
his hand. For the time being he doesn't love her. That's
clear! She is too something – extreme. In fact, she has
just been saying there's nothing lost in being extreme.
What you get is the expanded moment – wider, deeper.
But something is wrong. He is slamming the bedroom
door and the moment contracts. Now each of them is a
monster, violently different from the other. They have
done the dream of love to death! And then what happens
is the moment passes. She turns up the music.

Did I mention it's summer? ～

Part Two

A Bit of Sharp Eyeing

*Walking by, she knows her bare
legs are good.*

*If someone leaning against a brick wall
looks on, no problem.*

Otherwise a Blank Canvas

This picture is the most complex thing I have ever done. It's of me organizing the playroom. I know there's too much colour, too many detached limbs. But look in the top right-hand corner. That's where the children hover as a smudge of pink looking down on the scene like cherubim.

A striking part of the picture is the toy soldier lower right. He's making a speech to the dolls, stuffed animals, and assorted blocks of wood that are sitting on toy-size conference chairs. The key to the security of the playroom, he's telling them, is patrol ships, subs, a fleet of destroyers, and jets with missiles.

The donkey with the torn-off ear sitting in the front row taking notes is me. Have I got it right? There's the alleged threat to the playroom that must be countered and there's the playroom inhabitants wondering if they're even alive?

Everything else in the picture is a production: the wolf off-picture scratching at the playroom door to get in; the heavy dew that arrived the same time I began the picture and has never ceased blurring the edges; and the clueless soldier of fortune scurrying about in the overlit background. He's just been poisoned and is trying to find the antidote within the next half hour. ～

No Kidding!

They are calling for illness. They are saying things will
turn sour, that happiness will begin to cost. That it
begins in middle age when there'll be no new thoughts,
when relationships will be debated. Not only that, but
mental rain will not cease falling. Jokes may lead to
happy impact but the passion position will be mixed.
And there'll be bereavement every birthday. We will
sicken at the sight of a flaming cake. Furthermore, fat
youth will regularly knock us over. No one will invite us
to big, sweaty dance parties. And though social factors
will suggest we become a new bride or groom, it is
uncertain whether love will reduce our misery.

Who knew this train was coming? Oh the toothless
old! Watch out when you're on the tracks, they warn us.
That light heading your way isn't the full moon. ⌒

Espresso

When Leonard Cohen left Main Street he travelled by
train. He'd sit alone in a darkened car with the window
open. It was cold and silent and windy in there. Now
and then he'd toss a handful of words out the window
like they were scraps meant to feed hungry birds. People
started collecting the words and pasting them onto
coffee cups.

Years later he abandoned the train for the
cleanup crew.

Now he's wet mopping a barroom floor as patrons,
youngsters, and every Zen moment just drift away. He's
merry. He's smiling broadly. But we're still hungry, still
collecting his words and pasting them onto coffee cups.
There is considerable debate as to why this must be. ∽

Geese Like Carpet Bombers

We had a barn. And they would put up a white sheet
on the side of the barn and Mom had a projector. That's
how we watched movies in 1992.

As a result I have always felt like a small, cold guy
watching events from a dry field.

As a further result I now mainly focus on this box.
It contains a *National Geographic* picture of the full
moon set against a black sky; seventeen paint samples
to represent the many shades of dried grass; and another
picture, one of nine Canada geese flying like carpet
bombers in a movie about the Second World War.

But I'd rather be in another world, a car commercial
or something. ~

Wanting Cake

It's funny out today. There's a mild grin in the air.
It's like the chirping sparrows are really laughing
their heads off. Like the gulls overhead are cawing
ha, ha, ha. I don't know what's so funny. It's my
birthday. Is that what's funny?

As usual, I wind up at Mother's for my birthday
celebration. Mother is one of those special spring-
loaded ones. It's vital to weave in her influence here.
"Aren't you glad your days of youth are over?" she asks.

Two bottles of meal replacement later I am corralled
in the grocery store lineup behind old Harry and
wanting cake.

"Zora's without love or a dog," he tells me. "What
a laugh!" Zora was forty years ago for Harry.

Under Mother's influence, thoughts begin forming.
Lipstick and a hairdo from the days when I was flesh-
coloured is what I am thinking. Some old-fashioned
fertility to disarm Harry even if we're both overripe.
It's still the twenty-first century, you know. We're
nowhere else yet. ⬿

White Sheet over Old Idea

In the Museum of Last Words a film clip of Superman's foster father is playing in a repeating loop. He's watering the flowers at the side of his driveway. It's a black-and-white day on a suburban street. The flowers look like weeds.

A girl rides by on a bicycle and after that Superman's foster father clutches his chest, drops the hose, and falls to the ground. We hear his shocked whisper, "No!"

Superman with his superpowers is on a mission elsewhere. Too late, he will swoop down and take his foster father in his arms. His super cry will shatter worlds. He sounds like us, then – felled by comprehension. ◞

How Wondering Is Essential

I mention how moments of ecstasy leave me wondering
if I have a chemical imbalance.
    She says it's the same for her.
    I mention going berserk with exclamation marks from
just looking out the window.
    She says, "No way! Me, too."
    I mention abstinence from alcohol and caffeine,
and using supplements like fish oil and vitamin D
to strengthen my brain.
    She says, "Same here, plus flax."
    I mention simple, unadorned reality.
    She says, "Absolutely."
    We both mention rocks, raindrops, clouds, and birds,
especially birds.
    She mentions how she's always wondering.
    I mention how wondering is essential.
    She says she's wondering if the time to be
brilliant is now.
    I say, "It certainly is."
    She says, "Here goes," and gives me a red leather
pouch with a black stone inside.
    I say, "Thank you."
    She mentions the stone has been blessed by a
Native elder.
    I say, "No shit."
    She says, "Now we are sisters forever."
    I mention it's a prime moment but the soundtrack
is missing.
    She says she agrees and then whistles. ∽

How the Lighthouse Meant Something

We can't remember where we were going in such a hurry. Last I knew I was hearing one of my kids telling his friend, "I don't know what's worse, catching your parents having sex or smoking a joint."

After that it was an old guy having dinner with his still-lucid wife. That would be us. What will happen next? Madame Tussaud, herself a wax figure, said beware the three crows – accountant, lawyer, priest – but I go further. I say beware Virginia Woolf and her hopeless clarity. She said she meant nothing by the lighthouse but I've never believed her. That lighthouse is the unknown shining back at us. ∼

How Some Rewrite Their Epic Poems

We are all fine people here. The landscape is lovely and
the weather is soft. Someone is always on duty. Usually
it's the solver of problems and this is a nice touch.

At three the bell chimes and we gather for tea. The
evenings we weather. They're not always lush. Some
of us have candlelit dinners with our sane old wives.
Others rewrite their epic poems.

I don't know what is worse, a tumbling marriage,
an uplift bra, or a sane experience. Sleep can be bad.
I, for one, no longer dwell in fast times, urgent needs,
or confusing moments. For example, in the last dream
I remember I was overhearing nothing. ⁓

How Time Expands

Concerning the proper enforcement of customs, the sexual experience made into a son or a daughter will raise you straight from the ground. That's true! The committee in charge of existence confirms this. Just now they're strolling about the festival site wearing long green capes. Soon they'll be awarding first prize for best compliance.

I should win! I have a son *and* a daughter!

My competition disagrees. There's a broken statue called Lillian that has spawned a thousand pieces; there are owners of grandchildren who are playing bingo in an attempt to lengthen their lives; there's the celebrity dog Rin Tin Tin that is showing off by walking backwards on its hind legs; there's a short comic with lust on his lips occasioned by anyone's vagina.

And the winner is?

Rin Tin Tin ... because he is immortal.

Then clouds drift by. Meaning time expands to include this gentle madness. ⌣

How She Rations Herself

I was not expressing disadvantage by having a mild
helping of dinner. I love protein but I don't lose my
mind over it. This is a source of helping the world,
I think, a bonus. I'm not using things up. I'm rationing
myself – a bit of dinner here, a bit of lunch there. I may
not eat much but I'm not afraid to be small. I don't care
how big anything is nor do I think that way. I think
my thoughts in careful measure. My thoughts are not
bargain basement though I'm often accused of taking
my mind to the thrift store. But someone's got to pay
attention to the junk!

A few days ago I was, like, living in the broom closet.
Today is better, a day to appreciate the dog's supper,
which gives me cause for a moment's wonder. It's just
that I don't wish to take more of the world than my
share. I breathe shallow, walk sideways, ration wonder
whenever I can. ⁓

How Mixture Causes Relationships

I tell my kids, don't walk into a relationship like it was
a moving truck. Take your father and me. We didn't
offer ourselves as targets to God so why should you?
I'm not talking here about the strangeness of it all. Or
the remarkable story about my eating sauerkraut before
coming to bed. Just sex, which is something necessary
in one's life along with a knife and fork.

    I also tell my kids I can't stand relationships that
are not concentrated and they shouldn't either. That's
the beginning of selfish streets. Same for enhancing
a man or a woman's ineptitude by floating their
failures past your friends. I don't advise that, either.
First you'll be petulant, and then unnecessary in
someone's life. Finally – and here's the chaff – you'll be,
"So what?" People will say of you, "She's terrific. I can't
stand her." ~

How I Was Wearing the Hood That Day

It was his birthday and his speech was running sour.
Each of us had to become a famous old person like him,
he was saying, famous among a dozen people or so. This
was his advice from the age of ninety. We were drinking
apple juice cut with Sprite.

There was cake, a dozen people, his speech. You,
seated beside me, were still conscious, thank God. You
had cake crumbs on your jacket lapels and were doing
what you usually do at gatherings, enshrouding everyone
with a look. It fit nicely with what our friend was saying
about the possibility of a fog bank with evil intentions
appearing at any moment. Or was it a seagull flying over
dropping sorrow?

People said, "Oh now, not yet, mustn't dwell."

The times, I realized, are small because we are. Small,
then pop, they're gone. But then I looked out the window
and there it was, the great hooded spring!

I grabbed your arm and whispered, "I am so in
love with my piece of sidewalk!" To which you said
something like, "Good." Or was it "Good luck"? ∽

White Suit / Far-Off Reality

My father would fall into the past whenever he looked
through an open window. He'd be seeing a thin line of
beach there and a pale sky the same colour as his eyes.
There would be heat, too, and then the woman who was
his wife laughing before a hotel mirror, her white hands
with the red nails clutching a silver hairbrush.

Sometimes I would stand at the window beside
him. And take in the sparkling water, the Palm Tree
lounge on the patio serving sky and surf, the handsome
suitor wearing a white linen suit escorting the woman
to a table.

My father would be in the bar by then, not
wanted at the banquet. And the small girl that I was
would be brushing her hair before the mirror after
everyone had left. ⌒

Meetings That Mattered

The woman wore white lace gloves and for a while she
rode with me on a regular basis. I'd position my cab
outside the hotel where she worked and tell her each
time, "Thanks a lot for choosing me." There was a whiff
of madness about things when she appeared. It felt like
fertility was about to happen! At first I'd leaned against
the car hoping she'd take a second look, notice the
he-man I thought I was. This was years ago. I remember
it like a series of hallucinations, or like a title: "The Lady
with the Lace Gloves." For a while she was all that
mattered. I also remember telling a bald man with
a wet dog that I picked up at the beach around the same
time that I had an unfettered message of hope to impart.
I can't believe I thought that back then.

This was well before marrying Thelma. "Enjoy your
tomato," she said tonight, handing me my supper, those
fierce words meant to delight. ❧

Say the Words

At the wrap-up dinner for the Love Your Package
workshop the women delegates began standing on their
chairs and proclaiming, "I am short in stature and proud
of it!" Before long most everyone in the hall, including
the five-foot-seven cheaters, had stood on a chair except
me. It was plain by their stares what I was expected
to do. I stood on my chair. I said the words. The place
applauded. I have never known such acceptance.

There were a few tall women still seated, outcasts at
last. One in particular was crying, hunched over on her
chair trying to look small. I thought I'd walk over and
console her; after all it's hard to lose top billing. ～

Country Life

We're plain in our SUVs and track shoes. Plain driving
by all those trees, a couple of which are ours. Plain, too,
at the rural mailbox where there's a gathering of keys
and cars. Where there's a flyer from the local butcher.
Frozen bangers on sale, buy one get one free! Frozen
bangers like a little British story.

   Then it's home to weed the driveway and after
that, our tea. And wind in the rose bush of which
ownership is ours. And next door, banging on his
roof but otherwise invisible, the retired pilot bored
with staying put.

   Overhead, a hobby plane is chewing up the sky. There
are tiny clouds, too, scurrying by like maids off to polish
the silver. ∽

Canary

A fluttering in my stomach caused me to realize I was pregnant. I didn't question how this could happen at my age but immediately went shopping. There were things to buy for the new life.

Jane, accompanying me, pointed out a yellow electric blanket that would help with the incubation. I bought the blanket, wrapped myself in it, and lay on my bed. The new life was now inside a womb inside a womb.

What would this new life be? Later that day I had my answer. A canary erupted from beneath the covers and began singing. Then it hurried off. Its early-warning services were needed elsewhere, at the thin line separating where there is no life from where there is. ~

Pause and Repeat

We look forward to the comatose reverence that comes with Christmas.

The season begins in early November when time starts giving off a creaking sound. It's going through its annual process of hardening. Our shoulders roll inward then and our heads collapse onto our chests as if in avoidance or prayer. Some of us make slow, grimacing smiles, stretching our mouths as wide as we can, repeating this motion several times, and then pausing.

During the lead-up to Christmas we no longer suffer from lost English reserve and everyone tries to be quiet. Once achieved, we bring our lips together and forward as though kissing a baby and flutter our eyelashes as fast as we can. This signals the arrival of the cart filled with tinsel. It's drawn by Lula the Malamute wearing a hat of reindeer horns.

Her arrival completes the seasonal outline, the one that is meant to endure. And Jimmy in the red suit on the roof blowing his nose. ∼

Jackie's Little Town

In the hinterlands of single motherhood Jackie's
fantasies range from perplexing encounters to
daydreams about practically everyone and their dirty,
great secrets. She is chock full of great secrets and round
the clock she mothers two teenage daughters who are
like cats with out-of-control hormones.

At night Jackie wears earplugs to bed to muffle her
daughters' acts of self-gratification. Someone once told
her that whatever falls from heaven is yours. So far
this has only consisted of her daughters' extravagant
phone-sex bills.

Otherwise Jackie's little town is insufferably boring. ∼

This Was Not Supposed to Happen

Wearing a lab coat is like wearing Superman's cape. Once people see you in it, they believe you're very capable. They believe you have skills.

Especially when you're a person who is forty-two years old and trying to hit the reset button on his life. And you're living with your mom where it's challenging to have her riding shotgun, definitely a lot more difficult.

But this person only has to work for Lorne for five more years before he pays him back for the time he totalled his truck. Likewise, there are only five more years of living with his mom while he saves the money to do this. He's in her kitchen now, heating up tomato soup in the microwave. One day she's going to put up some shelves and start displaying some of her stuff, he thinks.

"I totally respect you," his mom shouts from the TV room. She's loving the lab coat. "You're the best guy! An absolute legend! The choir of my life!" ⤳

Out of Order

The choir was officially deconsecrated. The biblical
narrative was in lawyers' hands. The many angels who
had sought bankruptcy protection there had either
disappeared or died. Every stained glass window and
pew, every cross was auctioned off to the public for their
personal use. The church became home to damage and
mice. A sign on its door read Out of Order.

For a while the laid-off reverend played the tuba in the
gutted interior, the oratorio of Elijah, but no one came
to listen. The lit candles left in hope and remembrance
melted to nothing.

After that the building became a curiosity. Tours drove
by. People scoffed. "Were they out of their minds?"

Now we hear someone is writing a three-part mystery
about these events in which everything will be explained
in the end. ~

In Vain

They are speaking to each other in Vain, an old,
old language. He said, she said, neither one of
them listening.

In Vain the streets are paved with mirrors and the
mirrors reflect the sky. Instead of walking, people float
like clouds.

Waterfalls in Vain are brooks that refuse to fly. High
opinions are mountaintops with exalted names, mainly
his and hers.

This morning they were up there with the clouds and
the mountains in a Vain attempt at escape ... ❧

Nobody's Going to Sleep Tonight

The Muses have gone mad and are living as lady golfers
in Palm Springs, California. They could care less about
me. I've become like an amnesiac lost on the overpass.
What's an overpass? What am I? If you want to see the
Muses they'll be pushing golf carts around the courses
of Palm Springs, or walking through town, dragging
their fat dogs behind them. But don't expect them to
deliver inspiration. Come twilight they gather in bars
where the drinks are half-price and the peanuts are free.
Their only conversation concerns pars and birdies and
they aren't even close to the mythical kind.

In Palm Springs the clouds are invisible and the sky is
like a sheet of blank paper. Thrift stores sell ratty scrolls,
harps, and masks that once belonged to the Muses, but
demand is low, though a pet store bought a tragedy
mask and hung it in the window. Inside, a tragedy of
kittens in cages.

About all this the mad Muses are of no help to me.
Just now a busload of Japanese schoolgirls has arrived
and I have to arrange them in the Zen garden, one
schoolgirl to every ten thousand pebbles. It's all too
much. I once saw a dog dive underwater like a dolphin.
But even this event is failing to point the way. ❧

Today's Forecast

Nature will be impressed with you now. This can be a pleasant day for cameras, oil, gas, cosmetics, glamour industries, fishing, shoes, and the genius of others. Your feeling thing is strongly aroused.

In fact, today, you stand to gain some kind of marvellous beauty. Someone might be wonderful to you! Several sniffs of outside air could turn into a love song or a poem!

Today you will manage the common madness in your own good way. This might sound corny, but the afternoon is one for pharmaceuticals in the garden! ⌒

Part Three

Did anybody hear me sing today?

— CHARLES SIMIC

Chickens and Us

They sing in a foreign language like opera, I'm told.
A squawk is a kind of aria fugata.

Mostly they're like old men gathering in the meal
replacement aisle at Safeway. That's why Emily
Dickinson crossed the road, to speak with them
about death.

Kurt Vonnegut thought the chicken's chemical
makeup was hilarious. It reacts as if it was some kind of
puritanical harbinger of death, he said, and that's why it
keeps crossing the road. Kurt Vonnegut did a drawing
of a chicken's asshole that has since delighted many.

Chickens will peck each other to death. They can't help
themselves once there's a wound. They're like us that way.
They love the smell of blood.

Although shaped differently, the chicken's beak
works similar to a human's mouth, ingesting one small
truth at a time.

Chicken Little syndrome is the condition of hysteria
that results in paralysis. This happens when the sky falls
on a chicken, another way in which chickens are like us.

At a chicken funeral sad music is played while a
chicken relative carries the dead chicken wrapped in
tinfoil towards a brightly lit fast-food restaurant where
a rotisserie awaits.

A chicken brain is about the size of a man's thumbnail.
Like ours, it's not big but sufficient for their needs.

Unlike us, a chicken is without a love interest or a dog.

In my day, my father said, we didn't ask why the chicken crossed the road. Someone told us the chicken crossed the road, and that was good enough for us.

Ernest Hemingway said the chicken crossed the road to die. In the rain, he added, while writing several novels about this.

I cross the road because even though I am a boiling fowl I am still able to cross the road.

There are twenty-four billion chickens in the world and only one billion roads. What will happen next?

I found this question in a magazine: How do you know if you're a birder? The answer: You are a birder if you have ever faked your own death to attract vultures.

Someone must know about Hugh and me. ⌒

Last Amphibian Flees Calgary Airport

Mother died of pneumonia one week after her spare
oxygen tank was taken away during our flight to Toronto.
An attendant said the tank didn't have a regulator.
Mother was sixty-seven years old, had emphysema
and cardiopulmonary disease, and had been on oxygen
for ten years.

Our boy, Alvin, who is huge, got nasty. There's a hole
in Alvin's nature big enough for a truck to pass through.
He convulsed with a violent aversion to the flight
attendant. "You just don't take away a person's spare
oxygen tank!" They put us off the flight in Calgary.

So we were all worked up about that. It took everything
out of us and we were just about dying from hunting
down hope, and trust, and gleaming promise, not to
mention another oxygen tank. So there was failure.

Then Charlie took off after the Last Amphibian, which
is what he calls Alvin on account of his turning from a
sweet baby into a twelve-year-old canister of woe. Alvin
was heading for God knows where. My stepfather, Lance,
went with them.

I could not go on. I could not continue these
explorations. A local man gave Mother and me cherries
and a few roasted almonds while we waited for them to
return, which they eventually did, Alvin with two double
cheeseburgers, his usual reward for compliance.

I could not know then that I would contribute to
Mother's death. I should have known about the airline's

regulator rule but didn't. Mother's tank ran out and we had no spare. I was too worried about Alvin to worry about Mother. She seemed happy enough sucking on cherry pits.

It was next day in Emergency when I got another tank. By then Mother had pneumonia. Morbidly, some other time, I will go into detail about that. ⌒

Smooth

During the night I burst out of my fur. Before this
I'd been covered in it head to toe. It came off in an
explosion; chunks of brown fur lay on the sheets, the
bedroom floor, the dog's crate in the corner of the
room. The force of the explosion woke me up. I was
sweating but quickly realized the significance of what
had occurred. Losing the fur was an enormous thrill. It
was beyond a thrill; I have never known such happiness.
I had to tell someone. It was three fifteen in the morning.
I woke up my husband.

"Feel my arm!" I cried. He didn't stir. "Wake up! Feel
my arm! It's smooth!"

He rolled over. "What the hell?"

"Feel my arm! Feel my skin!" I was hysterical with joy.
"There's no fur. I'm free of it at last!"

He threw an arm my way and mumbled, "Yes, yes."

"Now feel my neck!" I urged. "There's no fur there
either!" This was so amazing!

He pawed my neck. "Do you realize what this means?"
I cried. "I am now a completely smooth woman!"

He touched my head. "Your head is bald, Olivia," he
said. "Bald as an egg. Better check your pubes."

"This is just like you to spoil my happiness," I cried.
"I finally achieve something of real importance in life and
you don't even congratulate me."

"Congratulations," he said. "But you're still bald."

"Do you realize how long I've waited to lose my fur?
How important it's been to me? How hard I've worked?
All the books I've read? All the visualizations I've done?"

"Was that what you were doing Saturday mornings?" he said.

"You know what I was doing Saturday mornings! I was attending my Shedding Your Fur workshop. Susan down the road lost her fur ages ago. And Lorna, and Mary, and Lynn, none of them have fur anymore. How do you think it's been for me, the only one of my friends still walking around fully furred? Can you even begin to imagine the pitying that's been going on behind my back? Can you?"

He was completely awake now, as was the dog that had come out of her crate and was sniffing the fur on the floor. "I've always liked you covered in fur," he said, raising himself on one elbow to look at me. "That's the woman I married. I'm too old for change. Did you check your pubes?"

"Raymond!"

"Well, did you?" he said.

"Here, on the most profound night of my life, when I have at last reached the furless state of being, all you can think about is my pubes?"

"I'm going to miss your fur," he said.

"You'll get used to it."

He got out of bed, picked up several patches of fur, and together with those lying on the sheets, arranged them on his pillow. "I think I'll go back to sleep now, Olivia," he said, nuzzling the fur sadly.

Too excited for sleep I lay in bed for the rest of the night thinking about tomorrow. Oh the world is mine now! ➤

Along the Way

I got a job working in a burial park. In administration,
doing payroll, ordering coffins, urns. On the day
I was hired, the owner gave me a tour. The grounds
were exactly like a park: rolling hills, a meadow, oak
trees, benches for sitting; the buildings were low and
painted green.

The one where the embalming took place had finished
corpses sitting in rocking chairs along one wall; others
were laid out on tables and being worked on by three
old men. The men wore grey smocks and didn't look
up. The floor was sawdust, the windows open. It was a
warm fall day.

The owner lay on a divan and asked me if I could tell
the difference between her and the cadavers. I couldn't.
The embalmers were that good.

At lunch we ate in another building – roast pork,
cherry pie. Besides the embalmers, equipment operators,
salesmen, and groundskeepers were there. Everyone was
jolly. I was to start the next day.

I could bring my dog. It was full-time work. I thought,
I'll do this over the winter; there'll be stories; I can write
them up in the spring.

On my way out, I met the caretaker who lived in a
cottage on the grounds. There was something odd about
her – what we used to call slow-witted. I thought this
because she moved and spoke so slowly. She showed me
her garden. In spite of or because of her slowness, she'd
made a beautiful display. Every flower was either blue

or white, the grass in front bright green. She had a slow-witted dog as well – slow-witted or old.

I began appreciating everything.

Overhead there was sky and light and clouds sliding by. There were squirrels, falling leaves, the dead in their final rocking chairs.

I thought, Maybe it's time to slow down. ❧

Our Spiritual Lives

We've seen stains on tea towels that look like Jesus
Christ's face so we know he exists. And we know that
dried seaweed can save the Douglas fir from extinction
so we hang dried seaweed from the tree's branches.

And the story about the woman estranged from the
banking industry is true. She lost all her money to fiscal
fraud and now her days are long and cold. So we pray
to the banking industry not to do the same thing to us.

But some people don't pray at all, believing the
practice to be old-fashioned. My friend Warren is
like that. He says he'd rather trust the presence of
hamburgers in his life to render it benign. He told
me this at a party.

Most people, though, believe that the greatest
prayer we will ever say for ourselves and our children
is that none of us falls from the sky or falls into a
grave too soon.

Children, of course, pray to shells brought back from
the beach for unexpected joy to visit. A woman I know
named Andrea Sumner does this, too. She arranges
shells along with rocks, feathers, and pieces of dried
kelp in a circle on her living-room rug and claims
good results.

Then there are people believing there are giants
everywhere. And there are. You and I are just not
one of them.

And in case you're wondering about all those composite
pictures tacked onto telephone poles in recent weeks? It's
Jesus Christ again. The pictures are meant to show what
he'd look like if he were alive today and sixty-nine years
old and lost. Like practically everyone we know. ∼

Once Again

I was having a makeover. Hair, face, clothes, personality.

The consultant, a man, said, "You are arrogant, self-righteous, and take up too much space."

I objected. "But I'm trying so hard to be small!"

"It's not working," he said.

I cried, like, five times over that. Like a four-hundred-foot-tall baby stomping around making a big mess. ⁓

The Favoured Form

The burn victim with the scarred head and face and with
a hole where his left ear should be has won the TV dance
contest, beating out the celebrity two-hundred-and-
seventy-one pound transsexual with a heart condition
and the woman whose arm and leg were severed in an
elevator accident.

    I cheered along with an audience of millions. "You
are the sweetest things!" Remembering it is kinder
to assume they are not deficient or decrepit or
damaged in any way.

    "I am so tired of it all," you said. ⮌

Back Then

People painted their houses yellow, pink, or turquoise
in the hope of attracting their straying young like
hummingbirds to a feeder.

And if you did something special your picture
appeared on the cover of a vinyl record. You'd be
wearing a blue taffeta gown and a string of pearls and
be seated at a piano that was located at the bottom of
an empty well.

And scientists! They were like nosy gods wanting to
know everything about you. They'd take a slice of your
brain using a tiny scalpel inserted through your ear.
Then they'd study the slice, marvelling at the quantity
of your black holes.

People back then liked to read small, happy, historical
messages while sitting on the toilet and imagine a
time they didn't live in. And everyone's dogs, even the
chinless Shih Tzus, would climb onto rooftops to gaze
at imaginary sheep.

Back then you'd hang out with Uncle Vern in the
mornings and pick strawberries until noon. Then you'd
walk along a dirt road that smelled of horse manure and
wild roses to buy a single cigarette from the old guy at
King Wah Grocery.

One time I ran into John heading to the store like me.
John was one of the funniest guys I knew, and he wasn't
saying much so I asked him what happened. And he
said, "Aw, who wants to be a comedian when there are
fantastic one-off clouds to look at?"

On that particular day it was magical. Everyone was
addicted to living and time was our methadone. ◞

Nearly There

There was a competition for the job of playing myself.
I saw the notice pinned to a tree. It said there'd be plenty
of shifts, the graveyard for sure, and that the applicant
should have a stomach for fear. It said the person
selected would be restless and lean, dreamy but sober,
loyal, and sane. It said forget about holidays, they
weren't in the cards, but there'd be a control on sorrow
so you could stay afloat. And a guarantee of love so you
wouldn't be alone. Work would absorb you but money
would not. Perks you'd invent as you hurried along.
Time would be generous until it ran out.

I decided to apply. It was the chance of a lifetime.
And now for the good news! I'm on the shortlist! ~

Story Interruptus

I rushed from the bedroom when I heard the dog cry out. There was a giant in the living room swinging her by the tail. The giant was as tall as a beanstalk and stood rooted like a tree. His head brushed the ceiling. I don't know how he got in the house. But there he was. I was mad because he was hurting the dog. She weighs sixty pounds and her tail is sensitive. The giant seemed to be one of those dim-witted ones so I rescued the dog easily by prying open the giant's hand.

"Unfurl your hand," I hollered. He seemed stunned by my authority.

Once released the dog crept into my arms and we lay together on the living-room floor. The giant stayed put.

I was comforting the dog when Manny Moss came in from the woodshed carrying his axe. He took in the giant, the dog, and me on the floor, and the way it was otherwise dark in the room. "Sorry," he said, "I didn't realize you were in a story." He turned to leave.

"No, wait!" I cried. "You can check out that beanstalk!"

He complied and the story quickly became romantic. We lost our dignity for a few minutes in front of the giant but, oh well. ◟

An Outpouring of Generous Abandonment

I had not guessed that Owen with his red moustache
and excellent teeth would begin to afflict me with
discussions of our future life together. His mother
should live with us!

He could probably see by my closed eyes and my
arms clasped tightly around my knees that I was
going through a severe mental struggle.

We were on the beach. I was wearing a well-fitted
jacket and a skirt of dull green.

A seagull passed high overhead with a loud "Ship
ahoy, ahoy!"

Owen's lips were red and full. Just then they were
perched on a whine. "Don't spoil everything, Tina!"

His frown was a little like the passing of a light cloud.

I remarked that a man whose mother likes herding
cattle through the living room can be a problem for a
wife. I was also thinking of Morris, who was absorbed
with his series of Icelandic pictures and would not
be bothered.

"What you propose would be fatal to my work," he had
said. Blood disappeared from my face then.

Later, in Merlin Wood, Owen advised me to keep
away from Morris. "You've been made too much of,"
he said, and reconfigured his mind to alter his idea of
me. I was wearing my white dress, the material running
to innumerable folds. I thought, Today our marriage has
edges; the long-haul tingling may be over.

Come evening we absorbed ourselves with our
hobbies, Owen studying cases of the sick to discover how
to be well, me studying the shapes that spills make on
the kitchen floor. "Look! There's Iceland!"

What I cannot determine are a lot of things, including
Owen's mother, who is standing in our driveway with
her herd of Angus cattle. ⌒

We're Having a Foxy Time Where Everyone Gets Dressed Up

"I like to be a little bit subversive, or a little bit tongue-in-cheek, or dangerously close to being too revealing."

"Are you humouring me because I'm an old man?"

"I'm just ticking off all the boxes in the good-person department. So, what'll it be? The banana costume or the gorilla mask?"

"I had a hard time letting go of Linda."

"Forget about Linda."

"I want something evil."

"A wasp? A zombie?"

"I'm not dead yet."

"Attaboy!" ~

Local Gossip

I've lost my mind! I'm certain I lost it on the path
through the woods. It's dull black and frayed at the
edges. It must have slipped out of my head while
I walked. I want it back for sentimental reasons.
It's comfortable and keeps me sane at night.

If you have found my mind, please return it.
It's of no possible use to you. Leave it on the big
rock next to the tree where the eagles nest. I will
ask no questions. Wearing someone else's mind
is a damn scary thing to do. It's like having a ghost
in your house. Like being a dishevelled man in
conversation with a dog. Like being a dwarf speaking
of the world with sick wonder. ∽

Her Advice

On the plus side she says she no longer fears the
thoughtless remarks of others, says she's too old to care
for another person's indiscretion, that she's heaved
herself out of the seduction of general worry, and that
she's enjoying the long-awaited fun of jumping down
the neck of any fool who might open his or her mouth.

She's also removed any stepping stones she can find
because there is no longer anywhere to go. She feels
especially good about slandering the damned. Hell, she
says, is a cardboard box filled with dated opinions.

Lately, looking in the mirror, she's noticed that her
eyes are the same colour as the firmament. ⌒

An Interesting Woman

Pearl says she's finally become an interesting woman. She's eighty-six years old and writing a play about two dead heroes having a conversation. Prometheus is one of them. She says we don't remember much about our lives, nobody does. But the dead, she says, remember everything.

Audrey is helping with the play by transcribing for ten dollars an hour. She's sixty-one years old, has a husband, a farm, and two pug dogs. Audrey says Pearl's I.Q. has become egg-yolk yellow and that this is the mark of a brilliant mind.

Pearl says, "I thank you, Audrey, for keeping my red essence going, something I am crazy about."

This gives us cause for optimism. At the end we hope to flutter like Pearl. Like monarch butterflies escaped from the net. Prometheus remembering all it meant. ⌒

Private Life

In the basement there's a grove of handsome men in
low-slung pants and a seven-foot fat man in a cheap
suit who keeps bawling, "These gentlemen will amplify
your darkness!"

An old guy sitting in a plastic deck chair acts as a guard.
He reads books, too.

By midnight he's touched up my thinking. One
becomes interested in the tiny dancing man who never
tires and in the row of living heads lining the basement
walls, each one representing rebirth should I be
so inclined.

I am inclined!

Pretty soon the moment backs up and finds me
dancing with a svelte man in the moonlight. Then we
are lying on the long lawn of summer, the place where
every man's lips are with their girlfriends. ᴗ

Bulletin

You're in some little kind of mood. Your lady friend,
Gina, wants to go abroad, view a pond with swans, speak
to a young intelligence about castles. And it's a real kick
in the pants to realize your life is at home with Rose.
But neither of them seems to understand your position.
You're getting old. In fairness this means a significant
amount of crying about there being not so long to go.

So, oh boy, you are there, but, okay.

A woman told you the way to stop crying is to focus
your eyes on something near at hand. It could be
anything, she said, the edge of a table, the inside of a
flower, sunlight on the carpet, the chewed fingernail
on your own hand. What happens, she said, is that you
return to the present moment. It's not this particular
moment that is giving you grief, she explained, but
something else – a thought inhabiting the past or the
future. In the present moment you will find there is
nothing to cry about. ❧

Over

We found a beach where you got out of your eager
face and into something tanned. There were boaters
whizzing by and we waved at them like everyone else.
From one of the boats my ex was looking good and he
also waved, which pleased me.

I was sitting on the shore beside your moneybelt
and my coat of hope watching you swim. Your
dimples and cupid lips were on show, leaving smart,
sexy, and beautiful to me.

Later you referred to woe caused by your wife,
and promised rainbows over our future back deck.

That summer we drank too much. Our pleasure
happened regularly and was not afraid of hard work.
But in the end it was the idea of rainbows that sank
the affair. ⌒

Things Blowing Over

One week into the three-week visit bad guest exchanges were multiplying like some cruel something. We tried hanging garlic from every doorway to clear the air, and when that didn't work tried making spectacular football saves off a pile of pillows hoping to impress the guests with our lighthearted spite.

After that there was the souvenir windy night, which we thought they'd admire but it, too, was a bust. In such an environment why would anyone expect my nervous collapse on day fifteen to entertain the guests?

Fortunately, the god of day eighteen showed up. He's a wonderful mechanic and good at making things blow over. It rained so light on day eighteen that we found hope enough to take the guests to visit the universe. That's where they snapped pictures of the god of swans brandishing her warning trumpet. The pictures turned out rimmed in silver. A success!

When the guests finally left we exchanged padded coat hangers and playing cards from Cairns, Australia. At the airport we cried and said, "Farewell and be kind."

Back home we put on tuxedos and jumped up and down. We drank champagne on the deck and watched the bubbles drift towards the blameless sky. ∽

The Smart Jam Is in Finance

The busy children are slinging rocks at passing seagulls,
cut-off dates at each other. They've dressed the dog in a
sweater, wrapped buttered bread around the cat's tail.

A withered woman with a hands-off approach runs for
the exit. That would be me, their mother. Excuse me, but
I want to beat them with a hard malacca cane!

At this juncture you lose your mind. Then the dad
returns with sanity. "Tame them with money!" he says.
And waves a wad of twenties, telling the children to
say please.

They pause in confusion but something is working.
"Please," they say.

To the dad I bow in reverence. Thank you, a thousand
thanks, and thanks again.

Now I am thinking of when we no longer have them.
When I'm living isolated, a kind of hermit, with twenty-
one goats and a sweet little horse. This thought goes
a long way. ❧

The Logic of a Dream

The dream in charge of clerical gestures winds toilet
paper around my neck and says it's time to perform
the ceremony. Naturally, it's a Sunday. On the count of
three the naked day steps forward, trembling, unsure
of being seen.

 As usual I have been somewhere else, adrift in the
effluent of my mind, most likely.

 But then a scroll unfurls from the office wall, telling
me to look outside through the window.

 That done I will now record what I have seen.
A cloud field made orange by the setting sun. A garden
scene with a yellow watering can. A naked collection
of trees. But no rain from our western regions.
No woolly mammoths. ⌒

The Prayer We Prefer

Give us the special, spiritual helmet that protects us
from panic whenever we feel vulnerable and alone.

Give us treats such as two bottles of Merlot, or more!
We'd be excited with that.

Give us bucketfuls of hurled-in-your-face money and
a strong dose of never mind when the money's gone.

Give us a steady run of parties even if most of the
parties are with the dog.

Give us each morning a sunrise to dazzle as if we
only had three and a half hours to go.

Give us ideas that don't roll over and play dead.

And everything that is not, like, thump-thumping
to nowhere and then it rains.

Above all give us a crack in our spiritual helmets
so that Leonard Cohen can get in. ◡

The Americans Will Not Save You for Christmas

Greetings, large black person.

I have captured you by the short rabbits.

I'm sure you will not mind if I remove your toenails
and leave them out on the desert floor for ants to eat!

Take my advice or I'll spank you a lot.

Quiet or I'll blow your throat up.

Darn, I will burn you into a BBQ chicken!

I have been scared silly too much lately.

I have knife scars more than the number of
your leg hairs.

How can you use my intestines as a gift?

Gun wounds again?

You darling, lousy guy!

You always use violence. ⌣

† *From English subtitles used in Hong Kong films.*

The Rockets of It

I am lucky to have had my moments; to have been
moved by word of mouth; to have grown up with
people who preferred stark awareness. This for me
is the rockets of it.

Furthermore, no one has yet appeared at my door
holding a gun, which counts for something.

Overall, my position is that things coming to quits
are actually things moving nicely along. Living is the
everyday prize, and wonder at the baby who somehow
knows how to. ❧

The Next Story

For the longest time our stories were about Jenny
on her front steps, about her patience, her heart and
stroke, and the bees she kept as a hobby. Then Jenny
died. Now there were hundreds of people in our front
yard chanting my name, "Louise! Louise!" Ralph came
out of the bath and stood beside me grinning. "You've
produced one onion, one son, and one daughter," he
said. "It looks like it'll be your story from here on in.
Congratulations!"

But one onion, one son, and one daughter? It seemed
so little. At first I thought the crowd was early-morning
carollers. It was like they were giving away attention: you
didn't have to earn it, pay for it, wish for it; it was free.

I noticed the entire Loud family from up the street
were there with their balloon art, balloons in the shapes
of waterfalls and alpine fluff. Others in the crowd had
packed up their troubles in old kit bags from the First
World War and were smiling, smiling, smiling. Everyone
believing the next story would get them to their eighties.
What pleasure! Georgia O'Keeffe was there with her
new boyfriend, sixty years younger and handsome as
a rake. And Federico Fellini linking arms with a pair
of dolled-up fat women. "Louise! Louise!" Leading the
chanting was Ed English, the local butcher.

I realized I was now a block from home, in some kind
of procession. Kids and wheelchairs lined the route.
Women in cycling shorts waved flags, a troop of Boy
Scouts saluted. This was phenomenal and breathtaking.
Ed English in his bloodstained apron pointed out the
direction of the podium.

We were moving east. Beside me Ralph carried the
red thought blanket. It had belonged to Jenny. Her

husband in his bee outfit had stepped forward with
it earlier. The Raj Quartet was accompanying us
playing Gershwin. Ingmar Bergman was there having
a laughing fit by the Wintons' bird bath, the first ever.
I began to feel handsome. There was turmoil, tears,
and congratulations from well-wishers.

Ralph, still damp from the bath, draped the red
thought blanket over my shoulders. I was being anointed.
The blanket trailed on the ground like a bridal veil.

Mick Jagger's family from the big hectoring sixties
were there and more bare breasts than you could
ever imagine. People having famous intestinal
problems came into view – Charles Darwin, Dwight
D. Eisenhower, Anaïs Nin. A feeling I recognized as
I own the sky overcame me. I could die happily now
in my slippers and red thought blanket.

Ralph held his arm around my waist as we walked.
There would be loving hugs for supper. We walked slowly,
the crowd with us, and so happy. Before long I could
see the podium. It was in Heather Simpson's front yard.
It looked like a garden sculpture, a heron standing on
one leg. Gigantic mauve orchids were there. Nino Rota
playing the theme song from *Il Bidone* was there.

I gave a leading laugh. I was expected to speak,
expected to impart the next story, the one about
the onion, the son, and the daughter. The crowd
still laughing, joyous, ushering in something,
I knew not what. ❧

Acknowledgements

Several stories in *The World Afloat* first
appeared in the following publications,
with thanks to their editors: *Geist, Rampike,
This Magazine*, and *Imaginarium 2013:
The Best Canadian Speculative Fiction*.

A special thank-you to Karl Siegler for,
once again, invaluable editorial advice; to
Kevin Williams for supporting the project;
and to Terry Farrant for everything else.

M.A.C. Farrant is the author of more than a dozen works of fiction, non-fiction, and memoir, including *The Strange Truth About Us: A Novel of Absence,* which was selected as a *Globe and Mail* Best Book for 2012. Her stage adaptation of *My Turquoise Years* premiered at Vancouver's Arts Club Theatre in 2013. She lives in North Saanich, British Columbia.

Photo by Barry Peterson